THE O.J. SIMPSON MURDERS

40/40 Hindsight

I0652777

40 Clues that show
who killed
Nicole Simpson &
Ron Goldman

and

40 Clues that show
why O.J. Simpson
was not convicted

Sam Dennis McDonough
Aka: Clue Master SDM

COPYRIGHT PAGE

I dedicate this book to everyone who searches for the truth and seeks justice.

THE O.J. SIMPSON MURDERS

40/40 Hindsight

40 Clues that show who killed Nicole Simpson & Ron Goldman

and

40 Clues that show why O.J. Simpson was not convicted

Sam Dennis McDonough
Aka: Clue Master SDM

Table of Contents

About This Book

Around midnight on a foggy summer evening in a wealthy Los Angeles suburb, a distressed Akita leads two strangers up the dark walkway of a well-kept townhouse. The dog stops in the enclosed front courtyard and looks straight ahead. The strangers look in the direction the dog is looking and cannot believe their eyes. Two bodies, badly bloodied, are sprawled outside the upscale townhouse.

They call the police to 875 S. Bundy Drive in Brentwood. A detective identifies one of the dead as Mrs. Nicole Brown Simpson, 35, ex-wife of football great and TV personality, O.J. Simpson. They later identify the other body as Mr. Ron Goldman, 25, a friend of Mrs. Simpson.

By first light, experienced Los Angeles detectives have found a trail of blood from the murder scene to the estate of O.J. Simpson. They find the victim's blood in Simpson's car, on his estate grounds, and in his home.

Who is O.J.? Simpson is a major celebrity in a city obsessed with celebrity. Even the detectives who quizzed him the next day, June 13, 1994, handled him gently, sidestepping difficult questions. By the end of day, O.J. Simpson will have given several different statements concerning his whereabouts at the time of the murders.

Is it possible that a football legend, with a remarkably positive public image, would brutally murder two people? This book, *40/40 Hindsight,* lists **40** of the most obvious **clues that show** who was the **killer of** Ron Goldman and Nicole Brown Simpson.

It then gives another **40 clues that tell why this jury** found Orenthal James Simpson not guilty of the murders.

Chapter 1: Clues Left by the Killer

On a cold November night in 2006, a father called his children by the fire in their large comfortable home.

DAD: Listen, my children! I want to tell you a story about your mother and me. I know we have never spoken about your mother's death in the 12 years since she died, but now is the time. That is because I have written a book that I hope someday is a television movie, wherein I tell the world that if I killed your mother, this is how I did it. Are there any questions?

BOY: Is there any evidence that you did it? **Were there any clues?**

DAD: Well, let me see. **Let me count the clues:**

1. The police found a trail of my blood and DNA at the murder scene, while leaving the murder scene, in my Ford Bronco, on my driveway, and two miles away from the murder scene at my home.

2. The police found my blood mixed with the DNA and blood of Nicole and a man in most of those same places.

3. The police found blood, hair, fiber, shoe and glove evidence at different places along the trail of blood.

Scientific evidence shows that it was my blood found at the murder scene. The odds of the DNA belonging to someone else are greater than one in 170 million.

At the Murder Scene

(875 S. Bundy Drive in Brentwood, a Los Angeles suburb)

4. The police found **DNA** from Ron Goldman's blood on the glove that slipped from O.J.'s hand at the murder scene.

5. Police found cotton **fibers** on the knit cap left at the murder scene consistent with those found in the Bronco carpet

6. The police found nine **hairs** with the same microscopic characteristics as O.J. Simpson inside the dark knit cap found at the feet of the slain Ron Goldman and on Ron Goldman's shirt.

7. The police found a **12-inch hair** matching Nicole's hair on one of the bloody gloves.

8. The police found **shoe prints** from an Italian-made Bruno Magli, size 12, Bruno Magli shoe and they found four blood drops just to the left of his bloody shoe prints.

9. The police found O.J.'s left Aris light **glove**, size XL, at the murder scene.

10. Nicole bought a pair of Aris Light XL gloves for O.J. in December 1990 at Bloomingdale's in New York. Simpson wore Aris Light gloves from 1990 to June 1994.

Leaving the Murder Scene

(O.J. hurries from the death scene to his Brentwood home)

11. Blood and enzyme tests revealed that blood found alongside a trail of **bloody shoeprints** leading from the murder scene matched O.J. Simpson's DNA.

12. Simpson's **DNA** matched three bloodstains found on the rear gate of Nicole's residence.

Inside O.J.'s Ford Bronco

13. Police found a Ford Bronco hurriedly parked in a haphazard angle outside O.J. Simpson's estate. Police found Simpson's **blood** inside the bronco's driver door, above the door handle, on the instrument panel, and on the steering.

14. Police found **DNA** evidence of O.J. and victim's blood inside his Ford on the console, door, steering wheel and carpeting.

15. **Blood** on the Bronco car's center console came from the **two victims and O.J. Simpson.**

16. Police found a partial **bloody shoe print** on the Bronco's carpet to the left of the break-pedal that match the bloody shoe print at Nicole's Condo.

17. Police found a **bloody shoe impression** on the Bronco carpet consistent with a Magli shoe, size 12.

From O.J.'s Car to His Residence

Blood Evidence:

18. Police found **blood** behind the Bronco on Rockingham.

19. Police found three more blood drops on the driveway leading to the front door of O.J. Simpson's residence.

Glove Evidence:

20. Within hours after the killings, police found a glove on O.J.'s estate, two miles from the crime scene that matched the extra large **bloody glove** found at the murder scene. **Police found the second glove** (Rockingham glove) near the same air-conditioning unit where earlier a witness heard three thumps.

21. Stains on the bloody glove found behind Simpson's guesthouse contained the DNA patterns of O.J. and the two victims. Most of this blood came from Goldman. In addition, police found hair with the same microscopic characteristics as the hair of Ron and Nicole.

Fiber Evidence:

22. Police found cotton fibers on the Rockingham glove consistent with those in the Bronco carpet.

Inside O.J. Simpson's Home

23. Police found five blood drops on the foyer and in **O.J. Simpson's master bedroom.**

24. Police found **Nicole's and O.J.'s DNA** on O.J.s dark colored #13 socks left on the floor in his master bedroom.

25. They also contained traces of the same blue-black clothing **fibers** found on Goldman's shirt.

Chapter 2:   O.J. Simpson's Behavior

26. Several reports to the police show O.J. Simpson had beaten Nicole severely in the past, to the point where she was in fear of her life. She told several friends, "Someday, O.J. will kill me."

27. Police found that on May 3, 1994, about **one month before the murders,** O.J. Simpson purchased a German-made folding **knife.** This simulated-bone handled knife had a manual locking blade. It was six inches long and 3/4" wide, which according to the coroner was likely the same kind of weapon used in the murders.

28. O.J. had a bad week in June 1994. Nicole and her friend are slashed to death on the same day O.J.'s **ex-wife rejected** his company at their daughter's dance recital. On that same day, **his girlfriend,** Paula Barbieri**, refused to answer** eight of his calls.

29. Phone records show that O.J. Simpson made a call on his car cell phone at 10:03 pm, a time he claimed to be in his backyard chipping golf balls, or packing, or sleeping.

30. Only two people could testify they saw O.J. Simpson between 9:35 and 10:55, during the time of the murders. They were witnesses who saw O.J. near the murder scene shortly after someone killed Ron Goldman and Nicole Simpson.

31. O.J. was not home from 10:25 to 10:55 while the limo driver waited to take him to the airport for his scheduled flight to Chicago. **The driver first saw O.J.** as he entered his front door at 10:55, about 30 minutes after the murders.

32. The police found a **trail of O.J.'s blood and his victim's DNA** at the scene where someone **knifed his ex-wife and a friend to death.** They found mixed blood leaving the murder scene, in his Ford Bronco, on his driveway, and two miles away from the murder scene in his own home. He had cut his finger to the bone around the same time of the knifing but could not remember exactly how or where it happened. A few days later, he wrote a suicide note and was on his way toward Mexico with money, a passport and disguise when the police began to follow. After his arrest, he cried himself to sleep in a jail cell. He was remorseful until it occurred to him that jurors in Los Angeles find millionaires and celebrities not guilty even when the prosecutor has a ton of evidence and the defense has only a pound of dirt. As it happened, O.J. was both rich and famous.

33. When the LA police told O.J. in Chicago on the morning after that someone killed Nicole, **he did not ask how, when, where or by whom.**

34. When arrested O.J. Simpson had a deep wound on his finger, three smaller cuts, seven abrasions, and scratches made by fingernails. He happened **to cut himself very badly on his left hand around the same time of the murders.**

35. When police asked how he cut his finger, O.J. at first said, "**I don't know.**" Later he said he cut it on his car cell phone. In later testimony, he said, "that while in Chicago he cut his middle finger badly when he smashed a water glass in grief after hearing of his ex-wife's death."

Chapter 3: Letters

36. Following is the text of undated letter from Nicole Brown Simpson to O.J. Simpson prior to their divorce in 1992. The letter was entered in the Civil Trial. O.J. testified he never received the letter.

Nicole's Letter to O.J. Simpson

O.J. –

I'd like you to keep this letter if we split, so that you'll always know why we split. I'd also like you to keep it if we stay together, as a reminder.

Right now I am so angry! I wish someone could explain all this to me. I see our marriage as a huge mistake & you don't.

I knew what went on in our relationship before we got married. I knew after 6 years that all the things I thought were going on -- were! All the things I gave in to -- all the "I'm sorry for thinking that" "I'm sorry for not believing you" -- "I'm sorry for not trusting you."

I made up with you all the time & even took the blame many times for your cheating. I know this took place because we fought about it a lot & even discussed it before we got married with my family & a minister.

OK before the marriage I lived with it & dealt with (illegible) mainly because you finally said that we weren't married at the time.

I assumed that your recurring nasty attitude & mean streak was to cover up your cheating & a general disrespect for women & a lack of manners!

I remember a long time ago a girlfriend of yours wrote you a letter -- she said well you aren't married yet so let's get together. Even she had the same idea of marriage as me. She believed that when you marry you wouldn't be going out anymore -- adultery is a very important thing.

It's one of the 1st 10 things I learned at Sunday school. You said it (illegible) some things you learn at school stick! And the 10 Comandments did!

I wanted to be a wonderful wife!

13

I believed you that it would finally be "you & me against the world" -- that people would be envious or in awe of us because we stuck through it & finally became one real couple.

I let my guard down -- I thought it was finally gonna be you & me -- you wanted a baby (so you said) & I wanted a baby -- then with each pound you were terrible. You gave me dirty looks of disgust -- said mean things to me at times about my appearance walked out on me & lied to me.

I remember one day my mom said "he actually thinks you can have a baby & not get fat."

I gained 10 to 15 lbs more that I should have with Sydney. Well that's by the book -- Most women gain twice that. It's not like it was that much -- but you made me feel so ugly! I've battled 10 lbs up & down the scale since I was 15 -- It was no more X-tra weight than was normal for me to be up -- I believe my mom -- you thought a baby weighs 7 lbs & the woman should gain 7 lbs. And had you read those books I got you on pregnancy you may have known that.

Talk about feeling alone.

In between Sydney & justin you say my clothes bothered you -- that my shoes were on the floor that I bugged you -- Wow that's so terrible! Try I had a low self esteem because since we got married I felt like the paragraph above.

There was also that time before Justin & after few months Sydney, I felt really good about how I got back into shape and we made out.

You beat the holy hell out of me & we lied at the X-ray lab & said I fell off a bike...Remember!?

Great for my self esteem.

And since Justin birth & the mad New Years Eve beat up. I just don't see how our stories compare -- I was so bad because I wore sweats & left shoes around & didn't keep a perfect house or comb my hair the way you liked it...or had dinner ready at the precise moment you walked through the door or that I just plain got on your nerves sometimes.

I just don't see how that compares to infidelity, wife beating verbal abuse I just don't think everybody goes through this

And if I wanted to hurt you or had it in me to be anything like the person you are -- I would have done so after the (illegible) incident. But I didn't even do it then. I called the cops to save my life whether you believe it or not. But I didn't pursue anything after that -- I didn't prosecute, I didn't call the press & I didn't make a big charade out of it. I waited for it to die down and asked for it to. But I've never loved you since or been the same.

It made me take a look at my life with you...my wonderful life with the superstar that wonderful man, O.J. Simpson the father of my kid...that husband of that terribly insecure (illegible)...the girl with no self esteem (illegible) of worth she must be (illegible) those things to with a guy like that.

I just believe that a relationship is based on trust -- and the last time I trusted you was at our wedding ceremony. it's just so hard for me to trust you again. Even though you say you're a different guy. That O.J. Simpson guy brought me alot of pain heatache -- I tried so hard with him.

I wanted so to be a good wife. But he never gave me a chance.

O.J.'s "Suicide Letter"

37. O.J. Simpson wrote this letter at his pal Robert Kardashian's home on June 15, two days after the murders. Police found the letter on June 17, 1994, shortly before O.J. Simpson's televised Bronco chase and arrest.

To whom it may concern:

First everyone understand nothing to do with Nicole's murder. I loved her, allways have and always will. If we had a promblem it's because I loved her so much. Recitly we came to the understanding that now we were'nt right for each other at least for now. Dispite our love we were different and thats why we murtually agreed to go our separate ways.

15

It was tough spitting for a second time but we both knew it was for the best. Inside I had no doubt that in the future we would be close as fiend or more. Unlike whats been in the press, Nicole + I had a great relationship for most of our lives together. Like all long term relationships, we had a few downs + ups.

I took the heat New Years 1989 because that what I was suppose to do I did not plea no contest for any other reason but to protect our privacy and was advise it would end the press hype.

I don't want to belabor knocking the press but I cant beleive what's being said. Most of it tottally made up. I know you have a job to do but as a last wish, please, please, leave my children in peace. Their lives will be tough enough.

I want to send my love and thanks to all my friends. I'm sorry I can't name every one of you. Especially A.C., Man, thanks for being in my life. The support and friendship I received from so many, Wayne Hughes, Louis Marx, Frank Olson, Marc Packer, Bender, Bobby Kardashian I wish we had spend more time together in recite years.

My golfing buddie, Hoss, Alan Austin, Mike, Craig, Bender, Wyler, Sandy, Jay, Donnie Sofer, thank for the fun.

All my teammatte over the years: Reggie, you were the soul of my pro career. Ahmad I never stop being proud of you. Marcus you got a great lady in Katherine Don't mess it up. Bobby Chandler thanks for always being there.

Skip + Kathy I love you guys without you I never would have made it this far. Marguerite thanks for those early years. We had some fun. Paula, what can I say, You are special I'm sorry we're not going to have our chanc. God brought you to me. as I leave, you'll be in my thoughts.

I think of my life and feel I'v done most of the right things. so why do I end up like this. I can't go on, no matter what the outcome people will look and point. I can't take that. I can't subject my children to that. This way they can move on with their lives. Please, if I'v done anything worthwhile in my life, let my kids live in peace from you (press).

I'v had a good life I'm proud of how I lived, my momma tought me to do un to other. I treated people the *way I wanted to be treated I'v always tried to be up + helpful so why is this happening? I'm sorry for the Goldman family. I know how much it hurts. Nicole and I had a good life together, all this press talk about a rocky relationship was no morr than what ever long term relationship experiences. All her friends will confirm that I'v been tottally loving and understanding of what she's been going through. At times I'v felt like a battered husband or boyfriend but I loved her, made that clear to everyone and would take whatever to make us work.*

Don't feel sorry for me. I'v had a great life made great friends. Please think of the real O.J. and not this lost person. Thank for making my life special I hope I help yours.

Peace + love O.J.

(Here, O.J. Simpson scrawled a happy face!)

Comments About O.J.'s Letter

38. If the reason for the suicide note was that O.J. could not live without Nicole, why did he not say so in his farewell note? **Nowhere does he say** or even vaguely imply in the note that **Nicole's death is why he wanted to end his life.** Not only does O.J. show no remorse for Nicole and her family, in the suicide letter O.J. says that God had brought his current girlfriend, Paula Barbieri, to him. He tells how sorry he is that they will not have their chance, implying that he will not be around to enjoy his time with Paula.

39. Simpson is self-absorbed; not the type of person who would kill himself over the loss of another human being, not even an ex-wife he loved off and on for 17 years.

O.J. portrays himself as unjustly accused, but nowhere does he say who else might have committed the crime. **Nor does he request at this time for the police to search for the "real" killer.**

The next 17 pages contain a detailed account of the crime and its aftermath. The facts and sequence of events are from trial records and from O.J. Simpson's own words. **All the Times are Approximate.**

Chapter 4:   The Crime

40. The scene is in the upscale and trendy neighborhood of Brentwood, Los Angeles, California.

The Crime Timeline

June 12, 1994

AM

(7:00) O.J. **Simpson's girlfriend, Paula Barbieri,** breaks off her relationship with O.J. by phone.

PM

(2:30) - Brian "Kato" Kaelin, a friend of Nicole and O.J., is living rent-free in a guesthouse on **O.J.'s Brentwood estate.** Talking casually, Simpson tells Kaelin, "He and Nicole aren't together anymore." Kaelin said O.J. was brooding and cursing over his ex-wife's sexual escapades; that he had recently seen Nicole having sex with a friend, Keith Z.

O.J. and Nicole's daughter, Sydney, was in a dance recital at the Paul Revere Middle School.

(4:30) - Nicole made it clear that O.J. was not welcome to sit with the family, and she did not invite him to the family dinner afterward. He was peeved, moved away, and watched the dance presentation away from the family.

(6:00) - O.J. and Nicole leave the recital separately. O.J. told Kato that he left "in a foul mood…stewing over his ex-wife's behavior."

(6:30 - 7:00) - Back home O.J. tells Kaelin that he was upset seeing Nicole wear a "tight dress" at his daughter's recital.

June 12, 1994

PM

(6:30 – 8:00) - Nicole and nine others, without O.J. Simpson, eat dinner at the Mezzaluna Restaurant in Brentwood, a few blocks from Nicole's condominium. Her friend, **waiter Ron Goldman,** is working, but he does not wait on their table.

(8:00) - Nicole and her children leave the Mezzaluna Restaurant and stop for ice cream on the way home.

(9:10) - O.J. and Kaelin go to McDonald's in O.J.'s Bentley.

(9:40) - O.J. and Kaelin return home from McDonalds with food and go into their separate homes. Kaelin testified that Simpson appeared "tired". He observed that **O.J. was wearing a dark blue, cotton sweat suit.**

(9:35) - **Nicole's mother, Juditha Brown** calls Mezzaluna to inquire if she left her eyeglasses at the restaurant. An employee puts the "lost" reading glasses into an envelope.

(9:37) – Juditha Brown calls Nicole and asks her to pick up the glasses in the morning. Her mother would be the last person known to speak with Nicole.

(9:43) - Nicole calls the restaurant and asks specifically for waiter Ron Goldman. Evidently, she asked him to deliver the prescription reading glasses to her that night.

(9:50) - Ron Goldman leaves the restaurant to take the glasses to Nicole. While leaving, he said that he planned to continue on to Baja Cantina in Marina Del Rey to meet some friends. (Presumably, he stopped at his apartment to shower and change clothes.)

(The following four pages present the author's hypothesis of the events on June 12, 1994; taken from trial testimony, the coroner's report and O.J. Simpson's own words)

June 12, 1994

PM

(10:03) - While killing time before his 11:45 flight to Chicago, O.J. Simpson phones his girlfriend but again gets no response. **This is O.J.s eighth call to Paula Barbieri since her early morning message that she was breaking off their relationship.**

(10:10) - Perhaps O.J. is upset by Paula's refusal to talk to him so he goes by Nicole's condominium to see what she is up to.

Simpson parks his car in the dark alley behind Nicole's condominium. He walks through a broken back gate and peaks into Nicole's window. **He sees a romantic scene inside with Nicole shoeless and wearing a short black cocktail dress.** Perhaps low lights in her living room, a collection of candles and romantic mood music playing on the radio reminds him of an earlier time when he peaked in the window and saw Nicole having sex with a male friend.

(10:15) O.J. returns to his car and dons the blue knit wool cap and gloves he keeps handy to ward off the chill on the golf course. He also takes a knife that he keeps in the Bronco…for protection against LA crazies.

(10:20) O.J. returns to Nicole's condominium, most likely to scare Nicole and run off any man who might be coming to see her while he is away in Chicago. He hides in the dark bushes and waits to see who might show up to visit with his ex-wife.

(10:20–10:25) - **Limo driver, Allan W. Park**, arrives early at the Rockingham Avenue gate to pick O.J. Simpson up for his scheduled 11:45 flight to Chicago. He decides to wait before ringing the bell. **Park testified that he did not see a Ford Bronco on Rockingham Avenue.** Then Allan Park talks off and on with his mother and with his boss by phone.

(10:30 – 10:35) - Meanwhile, at Nicole's condominium, a man happens to come up the walk to return the glasses that Nicole's mother had left at the restaurant where Goldman worked.

June 12, 1994

PM

(10:30 – 10:35) Simpson comes out of the darkness and **accuses the man of planning a sexual date with his ex-wife.** Goldman denies it.

Hearing the commotion outside, Nicole opens the front door of her townhouse and steps outside. **Nicole's Akita dog, Kato** emerges and gives Goldman a friendly tail wag. Seeing this, **O.J. screams at Goldman that he has visited his ex-wife many times before.**

Robert Heidstra, a neighbor of Nicole, hears a white man's voice hollering 'Hey! Hey! HEY!' Then he hears a black man's voice, followed by what seemed to be an argument.

Nicole tells O.J. to leave Ron alone. O.J., with knife in hand, delivers a nasty blow to Nicole's head, cutting her defensive right hand and knocking her against a post or on her front steps. She lies **face down, knocked unconscious.** The blow to the head not only knocks her out, it bruises her brain. Evidence of this is a bruise, nearly an inch in size, on the right side of her head. For the reddish-brown color to appear, **Nicole's heart would have pumped for a minute or so.**

(10:35 – 10:40) - Confined to a gated-in area, about six-feet by four-feet, O.J. attacks Goldman with a knife. Ron tries to defend himself, but in uncontrollable rage and with a knife, O.J. works with savage efficiency. He cuts Ron's hands and turns him around. **He then restrains Ron from behind stabbing him twice across the neck with parallel, non-lethal cuts. The next wounds are stabs to the head behind the left ear. They are vicious, twisting cuts shaped by Ron's efforts to get away. O.J. rips Ron's skin as he withdraws the knife from the body.** (It is likely that at about this time O.J.s left glove becomes wet with blood and slips to the ground where detectives later find it for evidence.) **While Ron lay on his back, the killer plunges his knife into Ron's heart and lung. These fatal wounds cause a quick death.**

PM - (10:35 – 10:40)

Leaving Ron lying in his own blood, Simpson returns to Nicole. Using the 6-inch knife, **he nicks her once and stabs her three times in the left side of the neck. It appears that O.J. stabbed with a single-edged knife as each wound has a blunt end and a sharp end.** The cuts are not severe enough to kill Nicole, but they do cause extensive bleeding and may explain the blood on the steps above her body.

Although Nicole is face-down and unconscious, the killer pins her to the ground, as evidenced by a mottled bruise on her lower back caused by the shoe sole of a strong, heavy person.

O.J. pulls Nicole's head back by her blond hair and slashes her throat from left to right. The cut is vicious. The knife slices through her carotid arteries, nearly cutting through one jugular vein and leaving the second jugular vein dangling. **The cut is clean. She bleeds to death.** It is unlikely that Nicole could resist while O.J. slashed her neck.

When **Simpson regains control of himself**, he realizes he is drenched in blood and holding a bloody knife.

(10:40-10:45) - O.J. runs from the murder scene back to his car in the alley. Before getting into the car, he strips down to his socks. **While pushing a shoe off, some blood from the shoe transfers to his sock.**

He then rolls his bloody dark blue clothes and the knife into a small pile. (I think O.J. then puts on clothes he keeps handy to play golf.) He flees in his Bronco as fast as he can to his home just two miles away.

(10:47) Heidstra, Nicole's neighbor, sees a "white SUV" come out of the dark, west of Bundy on Dorothy, stop at the corner, turn right, and speed away down Bundy.

(10:48) Jill Shively, another witness who lives near Nicole, sees a Bronco speed through a red light and nearly hit the side of a van. Shively recognizes the driver as O.J. Simpson when he sticks his head out the window to scream at the van driver, "Get out of the way!"

(10:47 - 10:55) – Park buzzes the house once more; then stops buzzing and pages his boss for instructions if he should wait longer or leave.

June 12, 1994

PM

(**10:52**) - Simpson arrives outside his estate and parks his car in such a hurry that the front wheels are on the curb and the back end is sticking out into the street. Evidently, O.J. sees the limo and decides to go onto his estate through a darkened, hidden path that takes him directly behind the guesthouses that his daughter and houseguest Kaelin occupy separately.

(**10:53**) - In his haste, **O.J. stumbles into an air conditioner behind Kaelin's room, making a terrific racket. In the process, he does not realize that he has dropped the second bloody glove. Meanwhile Kaelin is on the phone and mentions that he heard thumps on the wall outside his guesthouse.** He wonders if there is an earthquake.

(**10:53**) – **Allan Park sees a shadowy black figure, about 6-feet tall and 200 pounds, come from behind the guest houses.** The man walks across the driveway and enters the front door of O.J.'s house.

(**10:54**) – Kaelin ends his phone conversation, goes outside to investigate the noise, and sees the limo outside the gate

(**10:55**) - **Lights come on inside O.J.s house.** Park gets out of the car and again pages the house. **O.J. finally answers the gate's intercom and says he will be coming out shortly.**

(**10:56**) -- Meanwhile, Kaelin approaches Park and asks if O.J. overslept. Still concerned about the noise he also asks if Park felt an earthquake. The chauffeur said he had not.

(**11:05 – 11:10**) While Kato is talking to the limo driver, O.J. comes out of the house and tells them that he had overslept.

Park notices that **O.J. is sweating profusely. Kato said O.J. was trembling uncontrollably.** Park and Kato load five bags into the limo. Kato testified that **O.J. had a small black knapsack that he insisted on placing in the trunk himself.** (Did that knapsack contain his knife and bloody clothes? The bag turned up later after being missing for quite some time, but the contents have forever disappeared.)

24

June 12, 1994

PM

(11:15) - The limousine leaves for Los Angeles Airport and O.J. demands that the air conditioner be kept on high during the entire ride to the airport.

(11:35) - They arrive at the Los Angeles Airport.

(11:45) - O.J. Simpson boards American Airlines flight #668 to Chicago.

(10:55) – Meanwhile, an Akita has been barking frantically, trotting up and down the street in an agitated manner. On this foggy evening, Steven Schwab, who was walking his own dog, came across the distressed animal. The dog barked intermittently and wanted Schwab to follow it, but relented and followed Schwab home. There, Schwab noticed red matted fur on the dog's belly and paws.

(11:30) - A neighbor, Suka Boztepe, agrees to care for the dog overnight.

June 13, 1994 - AM

(12:00-12:05) - In the Boztepe home, the Akita paces back and forth, persisting in its restless behavior. Boztepe and his friend, Bettina Rasmussen, decide to walk the dog to calm it down.

(12:10) - The dog leads them to South Bundy Drive, number 875, where it stops and gazes down a dim, bushy pathway. **Following the dog's stare, they see the shape of someone lying at the foot of the steps** with part of the body sprawled under an iron fence.

(12:13) - The first LAPD officers to arrive at the scene walk up the footpath and see the prone body of a female. They then notice, a short distance away, the prone body of a male. They call headquarters.

(12:30) - Paramedics from a nearby fire station arrive and confirm that the man and woman lying on the ground are dead. By then, a patrol officer had established that the woman was Nicole Brown Simpson, the owner of the building and the ex-wife of O.J. Simpson, the retired football player and well-known sportscaster.

June 13, 1994

AM

(12:30) - Nicole is shoeless and braless; she is wearing only a black cocktail dress and black thong panties. (Some friends say this was Nicole's usual attire. Candles light her living room and romantic mood music is playing on the radio. That too was usual for her.)

No one knew who the man was. On the ground near his body lay a set of keys, a dark blue knit cap, a beeper, a blood-spattered white envelope, and an expensive bloodstained left-hand leather glove

(12:45) – The man's wallet identifies him as 25-year-old Ronald Lyle Goldman. He fought hard for his life, but he was no match against a crazed killer with a knife. The police found Ronald lying on his right side, with his eyes wide open. He had scrape marks on his face and blood clogged his nose. **Someone slashed his throat and stabbed him numerous times on his chest, back, and legs.** Apparently, the killer dragged Ron to the spot where he now laid dead.

Officers enter the house and come upon Nicole's two children, asleep upstairs.

(4:15) –**Meanwhile,** in Chicago, Simpson checks into the O'Hare Plaza Hotel.

(4:00 – 5:00) - **Detectives inspect the crime scene** and inside the condominium. Having positively identifying the woman as Mrs. Nicole Brown Simpson, detectives decide to notify O.J. Simpson, Nicole's ex-husband. They thought it would be insensitive if police knew about Nicole's death and the media is first to notify O.J. Moreover, they decide to go to O.J.s house to **see if anyone else is in danger.**

A patrol officer said he had been to the Simpson residence on Rockingham Avenue several times for **domestic assault.** Since O.J.'s estate is only two miles from the South Bundy crime scene all four, Lead Detective PhillipVannatter, Tom Lange, Ron Phillips, and Mark Fuhrman go to Simpson's residence.

June 13, 1994

AM

(5:00) - Lights are on upstairs and several vehicles are in the driveway indicating that someone is inside. **They see a 1994 white Ford Bronco with the front wheels on the curb and the back end sticking out in the street, as though someone had parked it in a hurry.**

(5:15) - A detective searches the perimeter of the residence and looks over the Ford Bronco with his flashlight. The detective assumes the Bronco is O.J.'s when he sees a package inside with the name Orenthol written on it.

(5:15 - 5:30) - Detectives see what would later prove to be **bloodstains in Simpson's Bronco and bloodstains leading away from the car and onto O.J.'s estate.** They try to find an open gate so they can enter the property and see if everyone in the house is safe. Unable to gain entrance, they call Westec Security (O.J. Simpson's security people.) Westec dispatches cars to the estate and give police the phone number to the house. They fail to get an answer and think about checking inside.

(5:35 – 5:40) - Having found traces of blood, the police feel there is an emergency, that **someone in the house may be injured**. Detective Fuhrman jumps the wall so the police can get inside. They ring the bell but get no response.

(5:40 – 5:50) - The detectives then go to the three small cottages located on the property. In the first cottage, a young man, Kaelin, says he is a friend and a houseguest of O.J. Simpson. They look, but see no blood on Kaelin or on his tennis shoes.

(5:50) - In another cottage, a young woman identifies herself as Arnelle Simpson, O.J.'s daughter. Arnelle and the detectives go to the main house to check on the occupants. She tells them that she believes her father is inside. She opens the front door with a key and the detectives are surprised there is no one inside the house.

(6:00) - Detective Fuhrman discovers a bloody right hand leather glove on the path adjacent to the air conditioner near Kalen's cabin. The killer must have dropped it while hurrying back to his residence.

June 13, 1994

AM

(6:00) - Police find that Simpson had flown to Chicago the previous night to attend a Hertz Rental Car Company convention. They call Simpson at the O'Hare Plaza Hotel. When informed that someone killed his wife, **Simpson did not ask how, when, or by whom.** Although apparently distraught at the news, and concerned about the welfare of his children, he did not seek details about Nicole.

Immediately after the police told O.J. of the tragedy at home he began making phone calls to L.A. from Chicago.

Being the ex-husband, O.J. Simpson was a potential suspect from the very beginning. Because there was no evidence that directly linked him to the crime scene at this time, he was not an actual suspect.

(6:21) - Detective Tom Lange phones Nicole's parents. He expresses his sorrow to the Brown family and tells them that someone murdered Nicole. Upon hearing this, Nicole's sister Denise screams hysterically, O.J. did it! O.J. killed her! I knew he was going to kill her!

Denise tells Detective Lange that O.J. threatened many times to kill Nicole **if he found her with another man.** Denise also tells the detectives **that O.J. had physically abused her sister throughout their marriage.**

(6:30) - O.J. Simpson checks out of the Chicago hotel; he is on his way to the airport for his flight back to Los Angeles.

(7:00) - Detective Vannatter **finds the stains on the driver's seat, steering wheel and console of the Ford Bronco are blood. He also discovers droplets of blood leading from the Bronco onto O.J. Simpson's estate.** Evidence found and collected at the scene lead police to believe that **O.J. could be the killer**. Detective Vannatter declares the area a crime scene and moves to get a warrant to search the house.

(7:41) - O.J. Simpson boards the next flight to Los Angeles and continues to keep in touch from the airplane. Among those he calls is **Attorney Howard Weitzman.**

June 13, 1994

AM

(9:10) – Coroner Investigator Claudine Ratcliffe officially identifies the body as Nicole Simpson and begins to examine her. She has cuts on her hands and someone hit her from behind with such force that it knocked her flat. **He then slashed her throat with such frenzy that he nearly decapitated her.** Never once did she step in any blood, not even her own. Her feet were spotlessly clean. The coroner sees bloody paw prints on her body and shoulders. **Nicole's dog apparently tried to revive his mistress, and when he could not he wandered into the street for help.**

(10:15) - The coroner turns her attention to the male victim. **Ron's defensive wounds on his hands shows that he put up quite a fight.**

(10:45) - A judge issues a search warrant for the O.J. Simpson estate.

(11:08) - Arriving home, Simpson finds a full-scale police investigation underway. Police have tape stretched across his front gate and tags mark bloodstains on the driveway.

(11:10) - Patrol Officer Don Thompson detains O.J. with handcuffs. While doing so, he notices that O.J. has a bandaged middle finger on his left hand. O.J. does not question or resist the handcuffs or the arrest.

(11:30) -Attorney Weitzman arrives and asks Detective Vannatter to remove the handcuffs from O.J. Simpson.

News cameras capture long-time friend, Attorney Robert Kardashian, walking away with bags that Simpson did not carry into his house._**Kardashian throws the bags into the trunk of his own car** while the police are busy elsewhere and do not interfere. **(Could it be that the knife and rolled up bloody clothes were in that bag?)**

(Shortly before noon) - With police escort, Weitzman accompanies O.J. downtown to the Los Angeles Police Department's Parker Center for an interview. After some discussion, **Simpson agrees to police interview without his attorney present.**

June 13, 1994

PM

The police had read O.J. Simpson his rights at his home and now again at police headquarters. Los Angeles police question him for more than 30 minutes. They ask O.J. about the deep cut on his left hand middle finger. **Initially he claimed not to know the source of the cut. Later in the interview, he suggested he cut his hand when he reached into his Bronco, and then reopened it when he broke a glass in his Chicago hotel room when told of Nicole's murder.**

Simpson insists that he was not involved in the killings at all. Now he must stick to his story or be a liar. Overall, the interview was remarkably inept. Officers did not ask obvious follow-up questions. Perhaps detectives did not want to make their celebrity uncomfortable. (The interview was so unhelpful that neither side chose to introduce it into evidence at the criminal trial.)

(5:25) - Coroner Ratcliffe notifies Fred Goldman, Ron's father, by telephone of his son's death.

Eventually, police accumulate enough evidence indicating Simpson's guilt in the murders that they seek and obtain a warrant for his arrest.

June 15 – Someone contacted Attorney Robert Shapiro on O.J. Simpson's behalf and O.J. named him lead defense lawyer, replacing Weitzman.

June 16 - Funerals held for Mrs. Nicole Brown Simpson and Mr. Ronald Goldman.

June 17, 1994

AM

(8:30) - The LAPD notifies Attorney Shapiro that they are ready to charge and arrest O.J. Simpson for the murders.

(11:00) - Under an agreement with Simpson and his attorney, O.J. was to turn himself in to police headquarters by ten o'clock on the morning of June 17th, the day following Nicole's funeral. When Simpson does not show by the agreed time, four police officers and his attorney go to O.J.'s Brentwood home.

June 17

PM

They soon find that he is staying at the home of friend, Attorney Robert Kardashian, and comforted by another long time friend, Al (A.C.) Cowlings. By the time the police arrive, **O.J. and Cowlings have fled in Cowlings' Bronco.** Since O.J. Simpson failed to show at headquarter he is a **wanted fugitive.**

(12:35) – Police Officers discover that Simpson left behind a letter. O.J. addressed the note: *To whom it may concern.* It has all the markings of a suicide letter. It ends, *Don't feel sorry for me. I've had a great life, great friends. Please think of the real O. J. and not this lost person. Thanks for making my life special. I hope I helped yours. Peace and love, O. J."* Experts analyzed every word of the "farewell note" and they could only say that a guilty, distraught man wrote the note.

(5:56) - A motorist in Orange County notifies police that he saw O.J. Simpson riding in a white Bronco with a friend driving. They are about 60 miles south of O.J.'s house. Soon a caravan of police cars and a few curious drivers follow the slow-speed Bronco down the five-lane freeway.

At the head of the convoy, a suicidal O.J. Simpson, football star turned broadcaster turned murder suspect sat in the passenger seat holding a loaded pistol as Cowling drove. Onlookers jam the overpasses and cheer O.J. Simpson from embankments along the shoulder of the freeway.

Cameramen in helicopters fluttering noisily overhead provide live television coverage, **some showing Simpson holding a pistol to his head.**

The Ford Bronco continues, hazard lights flashing, into the city of Los Angeles, heading west towards the Pacific Ocean and finally come to a halt in the cobblestone driveway of O.J. Simpson's home. Police wait for Simpson at his home while news and police helicopters keep watch.

O.J.'s Arrest and Apology to Police

(8:51) - Finally, hours after the slow car chase began, 46 year-old O.J. Simpson, clutching a family photo, puts down his gun and steps out of the Bronco at the front door of his Brentwood home. Instead of rushing to put him in handcuffs, the police embrace him. Police allow O.J. to walk inside, use the bathroom, drink some orange juice, and call his mother.

In Cowling's vehicle, police find $8,750 in cash, a false goatee and mustache, a loaded Smith and Wesson .357 magnum gun, family pictures and a passport.

(Although O.J. Simpson had a loaded weapon, reportedly aimed at A.C. Cowling's head, and led authorities on a car chase, the police never filed charges for these illegal activities. **Cowling's friend, Jennifer Peace, testified that A.C. told her O.J. was heading to Mexico in the Bronco.)**

O.J. then walked back outside where he calmly apologized to the police. "I'm sorry for putting you guys out," he told officers "I'm sorry for making you do this." He shook a few hands, graciously smiled for the cameras and waved, as if taking a last curtain call before making his exit.

The Los Angeles Police arrest the former popular football running back and well-liked television pitchman **for double murder. They book him** at the LAPD Parker Center and put **Orenthal James Simpson** in jail without bail.

Chapter 5:   The Criminal Trail

1994

The LAPD gathers over 480 pieces of evidence. They present details to the defense, which has its own investigating team. **Neither the defense lawyers nor the police ever connect the deaths to drug dealers, hit men, or anyone else.**

July 8: Six-day preliminary hearing ends with Judge Kathleen Kennedy-Powell ruling there is **sufficient evidence for O.J. Simpson to stand trial on two counts of first-degree murder.**

The Power of Celebrity and Money

78. There was an unusual outpouring of **sympathy for O.J.** Admirers pinned notes of faith and love on his house gate and cheered their support on city streets.

77. Many qualified onlookers sensed a jury **acquitted O.J. Simpson because of his celebrity** status. People lose their minds over a television or movie star. That is just the way it is. They want to be on the side of the celebrity, the side of glamour.

Simpson's celebrity rather than money brought in the "dream team" of lawyers for his defense. They knew that defending O.J. against public prosecutors would bring fame.

40. - O.J. Simpson retained a team of very capable lawyers, including Attorney Robert **Shapiro** who brought on Alan **Dershowitz** and F. Lee **Bailey**. Then O.J. hired Johnnie **Cochran** who became the lead attorney. Henry **Lee** and Barry **Scheck** came aboard as blood and DNA experts.

Johnnie L. Cochran, Jr., friendly and well liked, mostly a local **civil lawyer;** he defends the rich and famous and may have never won a murder case before a jury. Johnnie Cochran, dealing from the bottom of the deck, played to the jury by injecting race into the Simpson case.

Robert Shapiro is a well-respected lawyer, known as a **plea bargainer**. His attempt to plea bargain a lesser sentence, if O.J. pled guilty, caused O.J. to name Johnnie Cochran his new Lead Attorney.

F. Lee Bailey, a nationally known experienced and perceptive **trial lawyer**. (Defended Patti Hearst in her bank robbery case; convicted.)

Alan Dershowitz, a nationally known Professor of Criminal Law at Harvard Law School and prominent **appellate lawyer**, chosen in the event of an appeal. (Professor Dershowitz secured a reversal, on appeal, of von Bulow's earlier conviction by a jury. He also defended hotel heiress Leona Helmsley on appeal and lost.)

Barry Scheck, DNA lawyer/technician. (In 1992, he and Peter Neufeld created the Cardozo Innocence PrO.J.ect. The PrO.J.ect uses DNA evidence to assist in overturning convictions of wrongly convicted inmates.)

Peter Neufeld, **DNA lawyer/technician.** (Co-founder, with Barry Scheck of the Innocence Project at Cardozo. Uses DNA evidence to assist wrongly convicted inmates in overturning their convictions.)

Dr. Henry Lee, forensic expert in blood splatters analysis.

Dr Michael Baden - forensic pathologist.

Gerald Uelman, was the defense team's quiet lawyer, a **former law-school dean.**

Jo-Ellan Dimitrius, defense jury consultant who chooses jurors scientifically.

Robert Blasier, a specialist in **DNA physical evidence,** and the only defense attorney to return for the civil trial.

1994

July 20: Goldman's mother files wrongful death lawsuit.

July 22: Judge Lance A. Ito will hear the case. O.J. Simpson answers the question, "How do you plead?" at his arraignment with, "Absolutely one hundred percent not guilty, Your Honor."

Aug 18: Defense counsel files motion to obtain personnel records of **Detective Mark Fuhrman.**

Sep 2: Motion filed to sequester the jury.

Sep 9: District attorney says the state **will not seek a death penalty.**

1994

Sep 19: Judge Ito upholds that search of Simpson's home was legal

Nov 3: Jury panel consists of eight women and four men.

Dec 8: Lawyers select an alternate jury.

1995

Jan 11: The jury is sequestered. A hearing held on admissibility of domestic-abuse evidence.

Jan 13: Prosecutor Christopher Darden and defense attorney Cochran argue over racist language regarding the **upcoming testimony of detective Mark Fuhrman.**

Monday, Jan 23, 1995: People of the State of California, Plaintiff, versus Orenthal James Simpson, Defendant, Case Number #BAO97211, Los Angeles County Superior Court.

Prosecution Opening Statement

Jan 24: Over the next 371 days, the prosecution would put 72 witnesses on the stand. They included relatives and friends of Nicole, friends of O J, and a 9-1-1 dispatcher.

Christopher Darden gives the prosecution's opening statement by portraying O.J. Simpson as an abusive husband and jealous of his ex-wife's new found loves. Simpson had been unable to reconcile himself to a life without Nicole while she had moved on with her life, forming relationships with men. Nicole and her family rejected O.J. Simpson and he could no longer control her.

Darden told the jurors that, *O.J. didn't kill her because he didn't love her anymore. O.J. killed her because he couldn't have her. If he couldn't have her, he didn't want anybody else to have her.* He said that beneath O.J.'s image as a star athlete and actor was a jealous batterer and a murderer. On the day of the murders, O.J. made eight unanswered calls to his girlfriend who broke off their relationship that morning. Perhaps Paula's refusal to talk so upset him that he decided to go by Nicole's condominium to see what she was doing.

Marcia Clark then described a jealous O.J. Simpson who stalked his ex-wife and her activities. She said there was a path of blood leading from the murder scene on Bundy, in O.J.'s Ford Bronco, and into his Rockingham home. There is devastating DNA proof that it was O.J. Simpson alone who killed these two people in a fit of jealous rage.

The witnesses suggested that O.J. had the **motive and the opportunity** to kill his ex-wife and her friend. The first set of witnesses gave evidence of O.J.'s motives: his **jealousy and history of domestic abuse.** The next set of witnesses that included Allan Park, Kato Kaelin, and officers of the LAPD established a timeline of events that would show that O.J. Simpson had in fact used his **opportunity to kill**

Defense Opening Statement

Jan 25: - The opening statement for the defense stated their central themes: **The prosecution's rush to judgment and their obsession to win at all costs.** Cochran then presented his timeline of events and he suggested that Simpson, so crippled by arthritis, could not have possibly pulled off a double murder. He said the defense would prove the state's DNA evidence against O.J. Simpson was **contaminated and the police compromised and corrupted other evidence.**

Johnnie Cochran addressed the mostly African-American jury by quoting from Martin Luther King Jr., "Injustice anywhere is a threat to justice everywhere." He then reminded the **largely black jury that they were the conscience of their community and that when the trial was over they had to return there.**

Jan 27: Simpson publishes his book: *I Want to Tell You.*

Case for the Prosecution

Jan 31: The prosecution calls a 9-1-1 dispatcher to the stand so they could play for the jury a terrifying call from Nicole describing an ongoing assault by Simpson. She shouted into the phone: *When he gets this crazed, I get scared. He gets a very animalistic look in him. His eyes are black, just black; I mean cold, like an animal.*

1995

Detective John Edwards responded to a 911 call on New Year's Day 1989. He testified that a severely beaten Nicole Brown Simpson ran from the bushes wearing only a bra and sweatpants, crying, *He's going to kill me. He's going to kill me.* She said O.J. had beaten her badly. Her face showed a cut lip, a swollen and blackened left eye and cheek." He also saw a hand imprint on her neck.

Feb 3: Denise testified how O.J. Simpson abused her sister. She told of a dinner attended by her, Nicole and friends when O.J. grabbed Nicole's crotch and said, "This is where babies come from, and it belongs to me."

Feb 7: Finally, the prosecution put on witnesses **directly tying O.J. to the two murders.** The evidence related mostly to the results of blood, hair, fiber, shoe print and glove analysis from the crime scene and from O.J. Simpson's car and home.

The most compelling testimony concerned two Restriction Fragment Length Polymorphism (RFLP) tests. The first indicated that blood found at the crime scene could have come from one of 170 million sources of blood, and that O.J. was the one that fit the profile. The second came from DNA found on socks at the foot of O J's bed. The prosecution said only 1 out of 6.8 billion sources of blood matched the sample. **Nicole could be the only person on earth whose blood matched blood found on O.J.'s socks.**

On cross-examination, the defense had little choice but to develop theories that corrupt police officers either **contaminated or planted the blood sources.** They decided to charge ahead with both.

The court agreed to a trip to O.J.s home so the jury can see the scene for themselves. Taking the trip are the judge, jury, O.J. Simpson, lawyers for both sides, and several trailing media types. The defense sees it as an opportunity to put a favorable spin on O.J. Simpson's life.

Feb 12: - Someone had replaced pictures of O.J.'s girlfriend with a Norman Rockwell print depicting Federal Marshals escorting a black girl to school and pictures of O.J. and white golfers with pictures of his mother and other black people. They placed a Bible on a living room table.

1995

The scene shows how the defense early on in the trial was playing to a jury that now included nine blacks. As the group toured, O.J. pointed to a backyard play area and said, "That's where I practiced my golf swing." However, "in-control" O.J. was angry that the flagpole had no flag.

Mar 9-16: - The most talked-about aspect of the defense case concerned Mark Fuhrman, the LAPD detective who found the bloody glove outside Kato Kaelin's cottage.

Apr 11: - Under cross-examination by defense attorney Barry Scheck, LAPD criminalist Dennis Fung concedes many procedural errors.

May 4: - Wrongful death suit filed on behalf of Goldman.

May 10: - Henry Lee, a soft-spoken Chinese-American forensic expert, smiled at the jury and provided a plausible justification for questioning the prosecution's key **physical DNA evidence.** Lee raised doubts with the jury with his simple theories about DNA tests, blood splatter demonstration, and shoe print evidence suggesting that there was more than one killer.

June 12: - On the anniversary of the killings, the Brown family sues O.J. Simpson for the wrongful death of Nicole.

June 15: - Prosecutor **Darden was confident that the bloody gloves belonged to O.J. Simpson.** He decided to make a dramatic courtroom demonstration by asking O.J., in full view of the jury, to try on the gloves worn by Nicole's killer. Judge Ito asked a bailiff to escort Simpson near the jury box.

Darden instructed Simpson, "Pull them on, pull them on." Simpson seemed to struggle with the gloves that the police found on his property and at the crime scene. Standing before the jury, the defendant grimaces and says they don't fit, and then said, *They don't fit. See, they don't fit.* The dramatic demonstration bolsters defense allegations that police framed O.J. by planting evidence. It would turn out there were three good reasons why gloves did not fit.

(1) The gloves were too tight for O.J. to put on over the **latex-gloves that the defense demanded he wear.**

(2) **O.J. was opening his hand** while putting the glove on giving the impression that the gloves did not fit.

(3) They may have shrunk due to being **blood-soaked**.

The defense did their damage. Later, Cochran would reuse a quip he used several times earlier in the trial in relation to other points in his closing arguments, the memorable refrain, *If it doesn't fit, you must acquit.*

July 6: - The prosecution rests.

Defense Strategy

Simpson's defense team strategy was to undermine the prosecution's ton of evidence with theories of police conspiracy and incompetence. They raised doubts about the prosecution's timeline and suggested that the key physical **evidence against O.J. was either contaminated, planted, or both.** They suggested that football injuries and rheumatoid arthritis made O.J. physically incapable of committing the murders.

Jul 10: - The defense calls its first witness, Arnelle Simpson, O.J. Simpson's daughter. Later, O.J.'s sister and mother would take the stand. By the time Simpson's mother finished her testimony, it was apparent to some courtroom observers that **jury members were showing more empathy for the Simpson family** than for victim's families.

Aug 29: - Judge allows the Fuhrman tapes played in court, with the jury absent. The tape plays Fuhrman using the word "nigger" while talking to a book ghostwriter.

Aug 31:- Judge Ito rules that the jury will hear two excerpts of the controversial tapes.

Sep 5: - The jury hears excerpts from the Fuhrman tapes. Mark Fuhrman turned out to be a godsend for the defense's "corrupt-police theory." Attorney F. Lee Bailey began a bullying cross-examination in which he asked the detective, whether, in the past ten years, he had ever used the *"n"* word. **Mark Fuhrman** replied, **"He absolutely had not.**

Fuhrman denied knowing or meeting a woman who claims he made racist comments to her. The truth is Mark used "the *n* word" many times, and it was on the woman's tape.

Laura Hart McKinny, an aspiring screenwriter from North Carolina, had hired Mark Fuhrman to consult with her on police issues for a script she was writing. McKinny taped her interviews with Fuhrman, who in addition to using the offensive racial slur disclosed that in drug related cases he had sometimes planted evidence to help secure convictions.

Obviously, the defense wanted McKinny on the stand, and they wanted the jury to hear selected portions of her tapes. The prosecution objected strenuously and argued that the defense never even suggested they had proof the police planted evidence so McKinny'testimony was irrelevant.

Judge Ito somewhat reluctantly, allowed the tapes as evidence. His decision opened the door for the defense to offer its fantastic theory that Detective Fuhrman took a glove from the Bundy crime scene, rubbed it in Nicole's blood, and then dropped it outside Kaelin's bedroom, to frame O.J. Simpson. Obviously, the defense intended from the very beginning to attack Mark Fuhrman and raise the race issue.

Sep 6: - With the jury absent, Mark Fuhrman appears on the stand. He refuses to answer questions, citing his Fifth Amendment privilege against self- incrimination.

Sep 7: - The defense asks Judge Ito to instruct the jury as to the reason for Fuhrman's nonappearance. Judge Ito agrees, but the prosecution objects. The question is under appeal.

Sep 7: O.J. Simpson will not testify on his own behalf. The public would not hear O.J. explain how he made a call at 10:03 pm on his car phone at a time he claimed to be in his backyard chipping balls, or packing, or sleeping.

Sep 8: - Appeals court rejects Judge Ito's jury instruction.

Sep 11: - Defense refuses to rest their case due to the unresolved question of the judge's instruction to the jury concerning Fuhrman. Judge Ito orders the prosecution to begin its rebuttal.

Sep 18: The prosecution conditionally rests its case.

1995

Sep 21: - Both the defense and prosecution rest their cases. In a statement waiving his right to testify, O.J. says, "I did not, could not, and would not have committed this crime." **He made his speech but he would not take the stand.** Other than the one sentence, Simpson said nothing at his criminal trial. Everyone wanted to hear O.J. tell in his own words what he was doing that night two people were murdered.

Prosecution Closing Arguments

Sep 27: - **Prosecutors deliver closing arguments.**

Marcia Clark's summation sought, among other things, to do damage control on the Fuhrman issue. Clark denounced Fuhrman as a racist and the "worst type" of cop, but, she told the jury, that does not mean there was a frame-up. She again took the jury through the prosecution's "mountain of evidence and trail of blood." She said Simpson dripped blood after wounding his finger with a knife during the murders. Scientific controls and testing by different labs thwarted any possibility of contamination or tampering. She reminded the jury again that DNA analysis identifies individuals with such accuracy that it excludes every other human being on the face of the earth except O.J. Simpson.

Christopher Darden then told the jury that O.J. Simpson could be "a great football player" and "a murderer" as well. Darden brought up the question of Simpson's missing bags. A few hours after the murders when O.J. returned from his hasty trip to Chicago, he carried bags into his house while his friend, Attorney Kardashian, threw a few bags **into the trunk of his own car.** News cameras captured Kardashian walking away with O.J.s bags without police interference.

Apparently, the bags have been in Kardashian's home since then. Except for the golf bag, all were empty. Kardashian says he never looked inside the bags and efforts to compel Kardashian to explain his unconcern failed because of his attorney status. Darden asked the jury, "Don't you want to know what was in that bag?" Could it be the **knife and bloody clothes?**

41

Defense Closing Arguments

1995

Sep 27-28: Defense Closing Arguments by **Barry Scheck:**

Scheck alleges the experts collected samples sloppily and handled them poorly, rendering DNA results unreliable. He raises the possibility that someone planted blood by taking it from a police crime lab vial that contained O.J.'s blood and a blood preservative. Most compelling was **bloodstains on paper wrapping** that should have held only dry blood.

Sep 27-28: -Defense Closing Arguments by **Johnnie Cochran:**

Johnnie Cochran compares Fuhrman to Hitler and his campaign against the Jews, saying: *there was another man not too long ago in this world who had those same views, who wanted to burn people, who had racist views, and ultimately had power over people in his country. People didn't care. People said he's crazy. He's just a half-baked painter. And they didn't do anything about it. This man, this scourge, became one of the worst people in the world, Adolph Hitler, because people didn't care, didn't stop him. He had the power over his racism and his anti-religionism. Nobody wanted to stop him...and so Fuhrman wants to take all black people now and burn them or bomb them. That's genocidal racism. Is that ethnic purity? We're paying this man's salary to espouse these views...*

Johnnie Cochran's summation for the defense added controversy to an already very controversial trial. His co-counsel, Robert Shapiro, later condemned his closing for "not only playing the race card, but playing it from the bottom of the deck," and for comparing Fuhrman to Hitler.

Every defense attorney knew from the beginning that Fuhrman would testify and that race would be an issue.

Some would call Johnnie Cochran the worst kind of racist.

Chapter 6   Jury Verdict

1995

Sep 29: The case goes to the jury.

This was a long trial with the jury sequestered for 265 days. Of course, they are showing signs of strain and exhaustion. Judge Ito was under attack for allowing the trial to drag on and for his seeming inability to keep lawyers under control.

Oct 2: After deliberating for **less than four hours,** the jury announced that it had reached a verdict.

Oct 3: As America watched at 10 am PST, Judge Ito's clerk announced the jury's verdict, *We the jury in the above entitled action, find the defendant, Orenthal James Simpson, **not guilty of the crime of murder.***

The jury had found O.J. not guilty on two counts of murder. After spending 473 days in jail, he was now a free man.

O.J. Simpson sighed in relief; Cochran pumped his fist and slapped Simpson on the back. Robert Kardashian, who may have known more about O.J.'s guilt than any one, looked surprised and stunned. The dream team gathered in a victory huddle.

From the audience came the searing moans of Kim Goldman and the cry of Ron's mother Patti Goldman, "Oh my God! Oh my God"!

The jury spent **less than four hours** deliberating a case that had produced 126 witnesses over 265 days and had cost $15 million to try. How could one of the longest trials in the history of America's judicial system produce a verdict after less than four hours of jury deliberation?

The O.J. case would bring fame and notoriety unmatched, even Defense lawyers become even greater celebrities. The **O.J. Simpson** verdict demonstrates the effects that celebrity and money can have on the judicial system.

1995

Oct 3: One juror, after four hours in the jury room, announced Simpson's acquittal, saying, *We've taken this case serious for nine months. It didn't take us nine more months to figure it out. We're not that ignorant.*

"I feel vindicated." O.J. Simpson maintains that the Los Angeles police planted evidence and tried to frame him.

Simpson announced after the verdict that the police should go out and look for the real killer of his ex-wife.

To show his concern, **his own "primary goal in life"** would be **to search for the killer** of his beloved Nicole. (Of course, he has made little effort to look, except in the mirror.)

In American justice, all too often, judicial procedures matter more than the truth. Justice is a game between the prosecutor and the defense to see which team has better debating skills. The rich and/or famous play the game with everything they possess.

Chapter 7 40 Clues Why Jurors Set O.J. Free

The prosecution's overwhelming physical and scientific evidence should have resulted in a conviction. How then could this injustice happen? The jury may have reached a "not guilty" decision because too much evidence confused them, they misunderstood the evidence, they were racially biased, or they could not grasp the meaning of circumstantial evidence or of reasonable doubt.

Jurors Looked for Reasons to Acquit

The forewoman and several other jurors said the defense team impressed them by efforts to raise reasonable doubt that Simpson committed the killings: Specifically, the lack of evidence and the lack of prosecution witness credibility.

41. Some jurors asserted that they shaped their verdict mostly by **their suspicions about the police and evidence handling.** Some said that Simpson "was being victimized by a racist police organization because he was black."

42. This jury looked for a reason to acquit. Three black female jurors, Armanda Cooley, Carrie Bess and Marsha Rubin-Jackson, wrote, *"Madam Foreman: A Rush to Judgment?"* Dove Books.

43. FACT: Among other things, the book reveals a jury seemingly hell-bent on acquittal and unmoved by the evidence. The jurors apparently **did not seek, nor ask any logical questions.**

44. FACT: If even one member of the jury really believed that even one witness in this case had attempted to frame O.J., that juror would have said so publicly. Immediately, there would be uproar nationwide and threats of riots throughout the country. Instead, the **juror's public comments** about their decision went something like this:

Police are Racist

M.R.J. writes, "*I don't put it past Fuhrman picking up all that stuff out there. I don't put it past [lead detective Philip] Vannatter trying to help-him.*"

45. Some jurors thought Detective Vannatter planted blood in O.J.'s home. However, Simpson admitted to Vannatter the day after the murders that he had cut his hand that night and walked around bleeding for some time. Why would Vannatter plant more of O.J.'s blood after **O.J. already told the police they might find his blood in his house?**

46. The prosecution was unable to make clear to this jury that "contamination" of a blood sample could not turn someone else's blood into Simpson's blood. However, the **jurors did believe the defense** that DNA results were unreliable because they were sloppily collected and poorly handled and that the police planted O.J.'s blood or tampered with it in a police crime lab.

47. Race was a factor early on and it clearly galvanized the jury. One juror said that Lead Detective Philip Vannatter "made misstatements" on the witness stand. However, nearly every juror emphasized that the racist Detective Fuhrman was the heart of the prosecution's case.

FACT: **No** one ever produced any **evidence of police misconduct.**

Detective Mark Fuhrman

48. Mark Fuhrman, the LAPD officer who found a bloody glove outside Kato Kaelin's bedroom, turned out to be a godsend for the defense's corrupt-police theory. Attorney F. Lee Bailey began a bullying cross-examination of Fuhrman in which he asked the detective, whether, in the past ten years, he had **ever used the "*n*" word.** Fuhrman replied that he absolutely did not. However, a tape recording exists of Mark Fuhrman using the word "nigger" while talking to a ghost book writer years ago. In response to the defense claim of a police frame-up, the prosecutor offered up a lame: **Yes, racist cops exist in the LAPD, but this case is not a frame-up.**

Some jurors said Detective **Fuhrman's initial testimony "did not look good for O.J.,** but later his role was critical."

49. C.B. - *"Fuhrman was the trial."* He then goes on to list a string of inaccuracies: *"Fuhrman found the hat* **[not true]***, Fuhrman found the glove* **[one of two]***, Fuhrman found the blood* **[only on the Bronco door, nowhere else]***, Fuhrman went over the gate [so!], Fuhrman did everything. When you throw it out, what case do you have? You've got reasonable doubt before you even get to the criminalists."*

FACT: At the time Fuhrman found the glove he did not know whether there were any witnesses, what time the murders happened, that fibers would be found in Simpson's Bronco, or whether O.J. had an alibi.

50. B.M.: *"Actually, we didn't touch on Fuhrman that much. I couldn't believe anything he would say. We didn't have a problem in that area."*

A.A.: added that since *"we know he is a liar, it was not necessary to deal with evidence he found."*

Juror C.B comments: *"Detective Fuhrman is a Racist. The defense showed that racist Fuhrman tried to frame Simpson."*

FACT: - Fuhrman's actual role in this case was minor compared to the other detectives.

Juror A.C.: *I did not like Fuhrman from the start. His breathing patterns shifted and, from where I was sitting, you could see him squirming. Fuhrman kept pushing his feet up against the backboard of the stand. You could tell there was just a little anger building up in him. I'm thinking that this man is lying."* She went on to say that when she *"saw Fuhrman, she knew he was a snake...he sort of looked like a Ku Klux Klan or a skinhead with hair. When I heard those things about the n-word, it was like a hot flash hit me. I didn't believe a word he said.*

A.C.: *A few jurors believed that Detective Fuhrman had planted evidence. I thought it was possible it was planted.*

51. FACT: Fuhrman could not have had enough knowledge about the murders to frame O.J. If every piece of evidence found by Fuhrman had been excluded, there would still be overwhelming evidence that any reasonable jury in the country would have found Simpson guilty. Unfortunately, for the victims, this jury was set to return an acquittal. Real evidence fell on their deaf ears.

FACT: O.J. Simpson was a hero to police when he played college football in Los Angeles. The LAPD always treated O.J. with kid gloves, even after his arrest. Why would five police detectives suddenly decide to perjure themselves and frame a man they admired and respected? Furthermore, if the police planted blood on the gate, as suggested by one juror, they would have ensured that the criminalist collected it right away. **What good is planted evidence if you do not make it part of the case?)**

The Jurors, however, insisted that **race played no role in their decision.**

Jurors Deny Race Factor in Verdict

The jurors deny race was a factor in their not guilty verdict. In *Madam Foremen*, the **three black juror authors** said when they finally got down to it their decision was not about race, domestic violence or Simpson's stature.

Prosecutor Darden is a Token Black

52. The jurors said they saw Christopher Darden as a token black placed at the counsel table by the district attorney.

Juror A.C. wrote:"I remember thinking he was there as a token because the jury was predominantly black," the forewoman wrote. *I thought the prosecution felt they needed this particular balance. To me, this was the first 'race card,' as it has come to be called, and it was played by the prosecution. It didn't fool me, and it didn't fool a lot of other people on the jury either.*

Domestic Abuse Not an Issue

53. Jurors did not consider domestic abuse:

B.M: One trial juror dismissed the issue of domestic violence. She said it was *a waste of time for the prosecution to show that Simpson's battering of Nicole provided a motive for the murder. This was a murder trial, not domestic abuse."*

If you want to get tried for domestic abuse, go in another courtroom and get tried for that."

O.J. Simpson's Gloves

54. RMB: "I think we didn't touch on another issue, and that was the effect of the gloves not fitting during the trial."

L.C.: In Madam Foreman, L.C. reveals that "I had a problem with the glove, and why it was there."

G.R. also had problems with the bloody glove, particularly regarding why there was no blood nearby.

C.B.: "Had the cut [on his hand] been as bad as they say it should have been, some of his blood should have been on the Rockingham glove somewhere, but none of his blood was on it."

FACT: Stains on the **bloody glove** found behind Simpson's guest house contained the **DNA patterns of O.J. and the two victims.**

DNA Evidence was Shaky

55. FACT: - Jurors that did mention DNA showed they were unable to understand DNA. One juror said that, *most of the evidence was DNA and that's what was so shaky.*

56. Prosecutors took weeks presenting strong physical and scientific evidence of blood DNA connecting Simpson to the crime. **DNA evidence, none of which was understood or believed by the jurors.** They could not follow the evidence and logic of DNA blood samples. Mostly, **jurors rationalized that the police mixed or planted blood** from O.J., Nicole, and Ron, even though the Defense did not introduce any such evidence in the trial.

Not Impressed by Prosecutors

57. Prosecution lawyers and witnesses did not impress jurors. Most jurors appeared not to be interested in what the prosecutors had to say and they believe prosecution witnesses were untruthful.

58. At least one juror believed Simpson probably committed the murder, but that the prosecution bungled the case.

Very Impressed by Defense Lawyers

59. From **Madam Foreman:** "Dr Henry Lee was a very impressive gentleman, highly intelligent, world-renowned. I had a lot of respect for Dr. Lee."

Juror L.C. said that the jury viewed Lee as "the most credible witness at the trial." "Dr Lee had a lot of impact."

A.C. writes **Simpson's doctor, Robert Huizenga** was "impressive, very knowledgeable, a very successful doctor. I believed him."

60. **FACT: The prosecution destroyed O.J.'s doctor on cross-examination**. In answer after answer, Huizenga struggled to shade his answers to help the defense.

61. Salute to O.J.: - Male **juror L.C.** flashed O.J. Simpson a black-power salute right after the verdict.

Not Enough Evidence

62. Some jurors thought the prosecution's case was weak and based only on circumstantial evidence.

A **29-year-old postal worker** said, *"If he committed such a bloody crime, then there should have been more blood in that Bronco than just this little speck that we saw."*

Forewoman A.C. thought it suspicious that the police found blood only *"after they had torn the inside of the car completely up, and therefore I felt it looked planted."*

63. FACT: Evidently, this jury was unable to visualize the trail of blood from the killing scene to O.J.s residence and inside his home.

Chapter 8 - If Jurors Threw Out :

64. If the Jury Threw Out the Fact That...:

Police found DNA from O.J. Simpson's blood at the **murder scene,** leaving the murder scene, **in his car, on his driveway** and in his **house two miles away** from the murder scene

If the jury threw out the fact that...:

In several different places, *O.J. Simpson's DNA blood mixed* with DNA of the murdered victims, Nicole Brown Simpson and Ron Goldman.

If the jury threw out the fact that...:

Police found blood, DNA, hair, fiber, shoe and glove evidence at different locations along the "trail of blood."

If the jury threw out the fact that...:

Police found nine hairs with the same microscopic characteristics as O.J. Simpson inside the dark knit cap at the feet of the slain Ron Goldman.

If the jury threw out the fact that...:

Police found hairs consistent with those of O.J.'s on Goldman's shirt.

If the jury threw out the fact that...:

The police found O.J. Simpson's bloody shoeprints at the murder scene. The killer left several bloody prints from size -12 Bruno Magli shoes (Simpson wore size 12). Blood drops near those prints indicate that the murderer injured his left hand or arm. Those drops, when subjected to DNA testing, matched Simpson's blood. (The odds are 1 in 170 million that it was O.J. Simpson's blood.)

If the jury threw out the fact that...:

Shoe prints found at Bundy were from a size 12, Bruno Magli shoe. O.J. owned size 12, Bruno Magli shoes.

If the jury threw out the fact that...:

Police found **O.J.s left Aris XL glove** at the murder scene.

If the jury threw out the fact that…:

The police found O.J.s right Aris light glove, size XL at his estate two miles away. Stains on the **bloody glove contained the DNA** patterns of O.J. and the two victims. Most of this blood came from Goldman.

If the jury threw out the fact that…:

Police found DNA from Ron Goldman's blood on the leather glove Simpson at the crime scene. It was one of only two hundred pairs ever sold in the U.S. A receipt showed that Nicole had purchased a pair four years earlier.

If the jury threw out the fact that…:

Nicole Brown testified that she bought the Aris Light XL gloves for O.J. Simpson in 1990 and there are photographs of Simpson wearing the gloves until the murders in 1994.

If the jury threw out the fact that…:

Simpson's DNA matches three bloodstains found on the rear gate of Nicole's residence.

If the jury threw out the fact that…:

Police found Simpson's Bronco parked haphazardly outside his estate. Witnesses say the driver left it there soon after the murders.

If the jury threw out the fact that…:

The police found Simpson's blood inside the bronco. It was inside the driver's door, above the door handle, on the instrument panel, and on the steering wheel.

If the jury threw out the fact that…:

Blood on the Bronco car's center console came from the **two victims and Simpson.**

If the jury threw out the fact that…:

The police found a partial **bloody shoe print** on the Ford's carpet just to the left of the brake pedal that matched O.J.s bloody prints at the murder scene.

If the jury threw out the fact that…:

The bloody shoe impression on the Bronco's carpet was consistent with a Magli shoe, size 12 worn by O.J. Simpson.

If the jury threw out the fact that…:

Nicole's and O.J.'s DNA in blood, were found on O.J.'s dark colored #13 socks, which were left on the floor in his master bedroom. They also contained traces of the same blue-black clothing fibers found on Goldman's shirt.

If the jury threw out the fact that…:

O.J. wants thinking people to believe this: that at about the very precise time a killer was slashing Nicole he **innocently cut himself very badly, and that he has absolutely no idea how it happened.** The cut all by itself tells us that this man is guilty of murdering these two poor, unfortunate people.

If the jury threw out the fact that…:

O.J. Simpson **did not turn himself in** at police headquarters as he had promised his attorney and the police that he would.

If the jury threw out the fact that…:

The defense did not attempt to explain why O.J. Simpson would make a call on his car cell phone at **10:03 PM, a time he claimed** to be in his backyard chipping golf balls, or packing for his trip, or just plain lying … in his bed.

If the jury threw out the fact that…:

O.J. Simpson could not account for his whereabouts between 9:35 pm and 10:55 pm on June 12, 1994, the night of the murders. O.J. said, "I was home alone and went upstairs at about that time"", I had a book in my lap and my TV was on, so I was just sort of spacing." **In fact, no one saw O.J. Simpson doing any of the activities** he claims he was doing during the time of the murders.

If the jury threw out the fact that…:

O.J. Simpson was not at home when the limo driver came to pick him up for his scheduled flight to Chicago. However, the driver did see O.J. enter the front door of his home about ½ hour after the murders.

If the jury threw out the fact that...:

O.J. Simpson beat Nicole savagely and she was in fear of her life at his hands. She told officer Edwards, *"He's going to kill me; he's going to kill me."* In a letter to O.J., Nicole wrote, *"You beat the holy hell out of me & we lied at the X-ray lab & said I fell off a bike ... Remember!??"* And later, *"I called the cops to save my life whether you believe it or not. But I didn't pursue anything after that -- I didn't prosecute, I didn't call the press..."*

If the jury threw out the fact that...:

Someone stabbed Nicole and her friend to death on the same day that **Nicole rejected O.J.'s company** at the dance recital and the same day his girlfriend was **rejecting his phone calls.**

If the jury threw out the fact that...:

Simpson had a strange reaction to the phone call informing him that someone killed Nicole. At no time did he seek any details from the detective regarding the death of the mother of his children. He did not ask how, when, where or who may have done such a terrible thing to someone that he said he "loved too much."

If the jury threw out the fact that...:

If he were innocent, O.J. Simpson would be outraged, **blazing mad at the police for charging him with murders he did not commit.** He would not return immediately from Chicago, he would not cry himself to sleep in a LA jail cell, he would not write suicide letters, and there would be no reason for O.J. to attempt an escape to Mexico. Instead, **he writes a note that reeks with guilt. No innocent person** would write such a note.

You could throw out the fact that...:

O.J. had **his passport** on him and was thinking of escaping to Mexico.

You could throw out the fact that...:

O.J. **Simpson held a loaded gun to his head** and threatened suicide during the slow-speed chase that took place at the end of his escape attempt.

You could throw out the fact that...:

Simpson had $8,750 in currency during his escape attempt.

You could throw out the fact that…:

O.J. had the disguise **while escaping in Cowlings' car**. If he bought the disguise for some innocent purpose, like, say, Halloween, why did he think it necessary to run with it.

You could throw out the fact that…:

O.J. had with him a disguise, a fake goatee and mustache.

You could throw out the fact that…:

O.J. bought the disguise less than three weeks before he murdered two people.

You could throw out the fact that…:

O.J. had a bottle of spirit gum, to put the disguise on.

You could throw out the fact that…:

O.J. had makeup adhesive remover, to remove the disguise.

You could throw out the fact that…:

While running from the police, O.J. Simpson had with him a travel bag that contained **extra clothing.**

You should throw out the theory that…:

O.J. says he bought the disguise to hide from the public. This comment from a man who says about his celebrity: "I love it when people recognize me on the street."

You should throw out the theory that…:

If the reason for O.J.s suicide note was that he could not live without Nicole, why did he not say so in his farewell note? Nowhere does O.J. say or even vaguely imply in the note that Nicole's death is why he wants to end his life.

You should throw out the theory that…:

The police framed O.J. Simpson. Simpson's defenders offer a wildly speculative theory that white people conspired to frame their man. If the police framed an innocent Simpson, why would he even think of escaping? O.J. Simpson, of all people, would know that every angry black person in this country would riot, if they really thought he were innocent.

65. Still **O.J. Simpson is guilty of the murders if we throw all the above evidence out and consider only the evidence below:**

O.J. Simpson just happens to have cut himself very badly around the very same time of the murders, and he just happens to have cut himself on his left hand. When asked how he'd cut it, Simpson first replied, "I don't know" and later, when pressed, said, "I have no idea, man." As Bugliosi points out, "That ridiculous statement shows an obvious consciousness of guilt."

The bloody **left-hand glove** found at the murder scene most likely fell during the knifing. Within hours after the killings, the police found O.J.'s **right-hand glove** on his estate near the air-conditioning unit where Kato heard a terrible racket the previous night. On this glove, police found DNA from O.J. and the two victims, they found hair with the same microscopic characteristics as Ron and Nicole, and they found a fiber matching those from the carpet of O.J.'s car. Most people, when they cut themselves badly stop the bleeding with a handkerchief. Soon they put on a bandage. They do not bleed at a friend's residence, in their car and all over their own house.

66. The **DNA evidence puts O.J.'s blood at the murder scene,** and that alone proves conclusively his guilt beyond all doubt.

O.J. Simpson shows no remorse for his ex-wife. In the suicide letter, O.J. says that God had brought his current girlfriend, Paula Barbieri, to him. He tells how sorry he is that they will not have their chance, implying that he will not be around to enjoy his time with Paula. Nowhere does O.J. say or even vaguely imply that Nicole's death is why he wants to end his life.

After the nationally televised chase, the police found a "To Whom It May Concern" note written by O.J.'s own hand. He wrote this after the police charged O.J. with murder, but before his escape attempt. Defense Attorney Shapiro said he had little doubt that it was a suicide note. However, the **prosecution chose not to submit the suicide note** into evidence that **"reeked" of guilt.**

Chapter 9   Jury VS Prosecutors

This jury refused to consider even one piece of the above physical, scientific, and circumstantial evidence in reaching their verdict. By ignoring every piece of evidence, they chose a verdict that reflects badly on America, Blacks, and the Jury System.

67. A Simpson quote: *Let's say I committed this crime…even if I did this, it would have to have been because I loved her very much…right?*

68. Jurors send most killers away for life if they find evidence from just one of these:

Trail of Blood

Hair evidence

Fiber evidence

Glove evidence

Shoe evidence

Attempt to flee.

O.J. Simpson's suicide note

Self-incriminating statement to police

Nicole Brown Simpson's letter of abuse

Witnesses who saw O.J. hurrying from the murder scene

Various statements about his whereabouts during murders

Various statements about how he cut his finger to the bone

69. Sworn to uphold the law, the O.J. **Simpson criminal jury**, driven by racially motivated lawyers decided instead to hold a private referendum on racism in the Los Angeles Police Department. This was not rocket science. **An honest verdict required only an honest right-thinking jury.** Neither O.J. nor his lawyers tried to explain how **Simpson's DNA was at the murder scene** and why **the victim's blood was inside his car and in his home.**

No one else on earth would have murdered these two young innocent people in such a hands-on brutal, savage way.

Over-Confident Prosecutors

The prosecution team decided to have a "downtown jury" instead of a "jury of Simpson's peers." They probably believed that **their case against O.J. Simpson was so strong** that even a more racially diverse downtown Los Angeles jury could see the overwhelming evidence against Simpson.

Prosecutors Ignore Expert Advice

Prosecutors ignored their jury consultant's advice, and dismissed them after the second day of jury selection. The jury **consultants had urged prosecutors to use their peremptory challenges**, to the extent that they might do so legally, to exclude blacks and females, especially black females. (Attorneys do not have to give a reason when using peremptory challenges.) The prosecution exercised only ten of their allotted twenty peremptory challenges.

It turns out that black females displayed a lot of hostility toward Prosecutor Marcia Clark. To Marcia Clark's credit, she honestly believed that black females would convict O.J. because of his domestic abuse. The "not guilty" verdict confirms that jury consultants were correct; that Black women were sympathetic to Simpson and less likely to convict.

70. The defense wisely made it difficult for prosecutors to challenge potential black jurors because California courts bar peremptory challenges to jurors based on race.

Original jury: 3 black, 5 white, 2 Hispanic, and 2 Asian.

The final jury: 8 black, 1 white, 2 Hispanic, and 1 Indian.

Before dismissals, original jury had 8 women and 4 men.

After dismissals, the final jury had 10 women and 2 men.

Jury Location

71. The prosecution's biggest mistake of the trial may have been to ignore their jury consultant's advice to have the trial in Santa Monica and **not file the Simpson case in downtown L.A.** The normal procedure would be to file in the judicial district in which the crime occurred, in this case, Santa Monica among O.J. Simpson's peers, mostly white upper-middle-class neighbors.

Most likely, jury location was a political decision. **Prosecutors may have feared** deadly racial protests, similar to a recent riot in downtown Los Angeles, after a largely white jury acquitted four white police officers of beating a black man after a long car chase. Poll data showed that most whites believe Simpson to be guilty and most blacks believed him to be not guilty. Prosecutors may have also believed that the expected "guilty verdict" by a downtown jury would have more credibility with the black community.

Jury Selection

72. The **defense team did a much better job picking "the right" jury members** than did the prosecution. Many legal experts think that the jury selection phase of the trial was crucial to the outcome; some think it decided the outcome.

The **defense made jury selection** process one of their main priorities. Jury Consultant Dmitrius collected and coordinated massive data on each of the jury finalists, including answers to questionnaires, responses and body language during voir dire. Among the criteria was ranking each juror according to sympathy toward the defense.

There may have been juror bias against the police, white people, or white women who marry black men and deserve what they get?

It seems that most jury members could not realize that DNA analysis identifies individuals with such accuracy that every other human being on earth can be excluded except O.J. Simpson. **Unable to grasp the value of DNA evidence; most discounted the blood evidence as unimportant.**

FACT: Prosecutors presented strong physical and scientific evidence of blood DNA connecting Simpson to the crime. It was only a matter of listening to the evidence and thinking.

The Race Card

A white lawyer who uses "race" in a criminal case is evil. A black lawyer who uses race is "brilliant."

73. This was a clear case of the black community sticking it to the LA police because of perceived past misconduct.

The truth is that it is exceedingly rare today for any police department in the United States to provide false evidence in order to prove someone guilty of a crime. In fact, the LAPD pampered O.J. in earlier allegations of domestic abuse. Celebrity and local hero O.J. Simpson would be the last black man the police would frame.

74. Every challenge by the prosecution of a potential black juror caused Cochran to approach the bench and suggest that the challenge may have been racially motivated. This tactic worked to dissuade the prosecution from challenging some black jurors. Everyone knew that the prosecution wanted white jurors and the defense wanted black jurors.

Trying on the Murder Gloves

75. Prosecutor Darden was confident that the bloody gloves belonged to O.J. Simpson so he decided to make a dramatic courtroom demonstration. He asked Simpson, in full view of the jury, to try on the gloves worn by the killer. Judge Ito asked a bailiff to escort Simpson to a position near the jury box. Darden instructed Simpson, "Pull them on, pull them on." O.J. seemed to struggle with the gloves, and then said, **"They don't fit. See?_They don't fit."** It would turn out that there were good reasons why they did not fit: the gloves may have shrunk because of the wet blood or they were too tight for O.J. to put on over the **latex-gloved hand the defense insisted O.J. should wear.**

The jury noted that this damaged the prosecution. Later, Cochran would reuse a quip he used several times earlier in the trial in relation to other points in his closing arguments; the memorable refrain, **"If it doesn't fit, you must acquit."**

"Framing" O.J. Simpson

76. If O.J. were innocent and he thought the police were framing him, he would not even think of escaping. He was a well known and highly respected TV personality and sports idol. He would know that the public, black and white, would demand proof of guilt and expose the frame-up, making him a world hero for exposing big city police.

If there were even one speck of evidence that even one person on the Los Angeles Police Force had attempted to frame O.J. Simpson for the murders, the media would have broadcast the event, as they say, 24/7. Black people, top politicians, and drug dealers would incite riots and make speeches demanding the firing of those in authority.

Women Jurors

77. The defense's research suggested that women: (1) were more likely to acquit; (2) did not respond well to Clark's style; (3) and that black women especially would not be as sympathetic to a victim who is a white woman. They saw her as a pushy, **aggressive white woman** who was trying to bring down a prominent black man. As a result, **the defense sought black women** for the jury.

78. Prosecutor Marcia Clark thought that women would sympathize with the <u>domestic violence</u> aspect of the case and that they would <u>connect with her</u> personally. She happened to be wrong on both counts.

The Judge

Judge Lance Ito was a star struck jurist who exercised little control over a trial that often ran amok.

Judge Ito allows Simpson's defense team to introduce fanciful theories of a top-to-bottom conspiracy.

Prosecutors Were Out-Lawyered

The defense team was professional and focused. They were always **a step or two ahead of prosecutors.** From the start, prosecutors were responding to the defense. **Using hindsight,** a few attorneys and others offered some reasons why this jury did not convict O.J. Simpson:

79. **The prosecutors:**

(1) botched a strong case through arrogance, negligence, and ineptitude. Prosecutors believed the murder took place at 10:15; a time not supported by the evidence. They insisted on charging first-degree murder, even though the evidence as presented fit a **second-degree charge** and may have resulted in a conviction.

(2) did not work hard enough covering the basics: interviewing witnesses, reviewing documents and preparing the police. Prosecutors should not have sought the death penalty. The evidence is that jurors who were not likely to choose **death were disproportionately black and female.**

(3) presented a case to the jury that was sometimes disorganized, disjointed, incoherent, and based on speculation instead of evidence. The strategy of presenting over 800 exhibits from 126 witnesses over 38 weeks confused the jurors causing the case to lose its impact. A methodical presentation by prosecutors would have left no doubt of O.J.'s guilt and would likely obtain a conviction, even from this hostile jury.

(4) could have and should have done a better job of presenting the evidence. When **the trial became focused more on police conduct** than on Simpson's guilt, the prosecution discarded some of the evidence collected by the Los Angeles Police.

The defense "opened the door" by trying to paint O.J. Simpson falsely as a leader in the black community. The prosecution should have made clear to the mostly African-American jury that **O.J. had done nothing to help less fortunate blacks.** Prosecutors should have presented evidence to show that the real O.J. Simpson is self-absorbed and is not the type of person who would care about any community, black or white.

Some Evidence Not Heard by Jurors:

80. Some key evidence that the prosecution, for whatever reason, failed to present before the court:

O.J. Simpson's Flight from Justice:

The **prosecution did not inform the jury** about Simpson's flight in his friend's Bronco, or that **O.J. held a gun to his own head** during the slow-speed chase. They also failed to tell the jury about the Police audiotape of their discussion with Simpson during the car chase as **O.J. was on the run from the police and contemplating suicide.**

They should have pointed out that O.J. had **clothing, a passport, several credit cards, a disguise kit, and $8,750** in the get-away car. Police found a receipt that showed O.J. bought disguise items two weeks before the murders. Thanks to prosecutors, jurors never had to consider why Simpson would need a disguise just prior to the murder of his ex-wife and Ron Goldman.

Cut Finger:

"How did you get the injury on your hand?" a detective asked Simpson the day after the murders. He responded, **"I don't know" and later, "I have no idea, man." The police made a taped interview that contained many inconsistencies and incriminating statements** that Simpson made to police about cutting his left middle finger the same night as the murders. The jury never heard this audiotape or his bizarre admission that he was bleeding all over his house right around the time of his wife's murder and that the very next day he did not know when, where, why, or how he cut his finger to the bone?

However, most people, when they cut themselves, stop the bleeding and soon bandage it. They do not bleed at the crime scene, in their get-away car, on their driveway and all over their house.

Simpson's Bruno Magli Shoes:

Photos showing Simpson wearing the size 12 Bruno Magli shoes turn up in one newspaper after another. This is proof that O.J. wore Magli shoes that he claimed not to own.

Stolen House Keys:

Police find Nicole's missing house keys in O.J. Simpson's possession.

Some Evidence Not Heard by Jurors:

Glove Photos:

The prosecution did not introduce photos and videos of O.J. Simpson wearing Aris Isotoner light leather gloves while he was a TV football commentator. The gloves are identical extra-thin leather, stitching pattern V-shaped vent at the wrist, and cashmere lining, to the bloody gloves found at the Bundy murder scene and on O.J.'s estate.

Knife Purchase:

Detectives found that on May 3, 1994, Simpson purchased a German-made folding knife from Ross Cutlery. This simulated-bone handled knife had a manual locking blade six inches long and 3/4" wide, which the coroner said was very likely the same kind of weapon used in the murders. The **court did not allow evidence of the knife purchase** because the owner of Ross Cutlery sold his story prior to testimony to the *National Enquirer* tabloid magazine.

Suicide Note:

After the nationally televised chase, the police found a "To Whom It May Concern" note written by O.J.'s own hand. O.J. wrote this after the police charged him with murder, but before his escape attempt. Defense Attorney Shapiro said he had little doubt that it was a suicide note. However, the **prosecution chose not to submit the suicide note** into evidence that **"reeked" of guilt**.

Crime Area Witnesses:

The Defense called Robert **Heidstra** to testify about hearing voices near Nicole's condominium during the time of the murders. A few minutes later he saw a "white SUV" come out of the dark, west of Bundy on Dorothy, stop at the corner, turn right, and speed away to the south on Bundy. Was it O.J. hurriedly leaving the murder scene?

Eyewitness **Jill Shively** did not testify because Marcia Clark felt that Shively was unreliable after she made an untrue statement to her. In addition, Shively sold her story prior to testimony to the Hard Copy TV show for $5,000. Shively says that while driving, around 10:45on the night of the murders, she saw OJ driving his white Bronco with the lights out going through the Bundy and San Vicente intersection.

Chapter 10 Civil Trial

O.J. says he will spend the rest of his life looking for the people who killed Nicole.

However, O.J. would soon be preoccupied with a civil trial.

Victim's Families File Wrongful-Death Suit.

On the anniversary of the killings, **June 12,1994,** the Brown family sued O.J. Simpson for the wrongful death of Nicole. On **July 20 1994,** Ron Goldman's family filed a **wrongful-death lawsuit**.

The Civil Jury consists of O.J. Simpson's Sana Monica peers who need only a "**preponderance of the evidence**" in order to convict.

1996

Oct 23: Jury of nine whites, one black, one Hispanic, and one person of mixed ancestry hear the opening statement. Judge Hiroshi Fujisaki proves he is no Lance Ito, and prevents Simpson's defense from introducing fanciful theories of a top-to-bottom conspiracy.

Nov 22: Simpson must testify in the civil trial and is before a jury for the first time. He takes the stand and clumsily tries to explain the unexplainable. He denies killing Ron Goldman or his former wife, but cannot explain the scientific evidence against him.

Dec 7: Juditha Brown, Nicole's mother, sobs while telling of her daughter's final days. She said she saw O.J. leaning over his ex-wife's coffin, kissing her and saying, "I'm so sorry, Nicki. I'm so sorry." Simpson was angry and in a foul mood at the recital four days earlier.

Juditha Brown says that in 1979, O.J. threatened to kill the Brown family if Nicole left him.

Dec 9: Ron's father and sister describe their family's loss: Ron blossomed from a shy youngster into an outgoing young man. He was a good-hearted, down-to-earth, hard worker who wanted to be a good friend, have a family, and be successful in the eyes of his family and friends.

Dec 20: An Orange County Judge awards O.J. custody of his children.

1997

Jan 16: Both sides rest. The Civil Trial Jury has heard 101 witnesses over 41 days of testimony.

Jan 21: In his closing argument, Attorney Daniel Petrocelli points at Simpson, "There's a killer in this courtroom."

Civil Trial Verdict: - Guilty of Murder

Feb 4: The trial would take just three months and would produce a very different result than the criminal trial.

A jury of O.J.'s peers deliberated 17 hours and using the preponderance of the evidence test, find that O.J. Simpson wrongfully caused the death of Ron Goldman and Nicole Brown Simpson. The jury orders O.J. to pay punitive damages of $25 million and compensatory damages of $8.5 million. (However, the award has proven to be virtually uncollectable.) In addition, under California law, O.J. can continue to survive on **$25,000-a-month** income from a judgment-proof $4,000,000 football pension fund.

Fred Goldman says *the family is grateful for this verdict of responsibility and for some justice for Ron and Nicole. The jury that acquitted O.J. was a travesty of justice that tarnished the criminal justice system. O.J. killed their son and the whole world knows it."*

Mar 26: Court orders O.J. Simpson to turn over his assets, including his 1968 Heisman trophy and a Warhol painting.

Jul 14: Sold at auction, the new owner of the Brentwood house soon has it demolished.

1999

May 10: O.J. Simpson and the Browns negotiate a custody arrangement for the two Simpson children.

2006 - November

After more than 12 years, there is **no evidence** to suggest that the killer was anyone other than Simpson. Later, O.J. would say publicly, "If I Did It, Here's How It Happened."

If, I Did It, a book by O.J. Simpson, set for publication by *Regan Books*, an imprint of HarperCollins Publishers. Publisher Judith Regan said O.J. approached her with the idea for the book, in which he hypothesizes how he would have killed his ex-wife and Goldman, if I did it. Word is that O.J.'s original title for the book was, *I Did It.*

Although Regan has acknowledged that Simpson does not directly say he was the killer, she said she considers the book to be his confession. In an interview promoting his book on Fox News, Simpson offered incriminating observations as, *I don't think any two people could be murdered without everybody being covered in blood.* (Fact: they were.)

A barrage of criticism met the announcement of the book. Ron Goldman's sister, Kim, expressed the outrage of the victims on CNN's Larry King Live, "*He's telling us one more time, 'I'm gonna continue to get away with killing your family members and I'm not gonna honor the judgment and look at me, ha, ha, ha.'*"

Of course, people are curious about what O.J. Simpson has to say, but **they wanted to hear him say it on the witness stand.** The criticism caused HarperCollins **to recall the book on Nov. 20, 2006, and Fox to cancel the Simpson interview.**

O.J. loves the attention and the fact that he got away with killing his ex-wife and her friend. Since he is unable to profit from his football fame, he is attempting to profit from two cruel murders that everyone knows he did. Just when you think he crawled under a rock and died; out he crawls to profit from killing Nicole and Goldman.

OJ Simpson is **making fools of the Los Angeles jury** that set him free, and all of the **black community** across the country that supported him.

Orenthal James Simpson took a knife

Plunged it forty times into a friend of his wife

But that's not the part that is so gory

He went to Fox News and sold his story.

O.J. Simpson lives in Florida on the $25,000-a-month income from a $4 million judgment-proof pension fund established when he played professional football.

There are no consequences. Simpson is not suffering, he is not in pain and he shows no remorse. Life is good to O.J.

O.J. is glad he got away with a horrific murder of an ex-wife and another white person. **He is glad not to pay** out to the real victims: the Goldman and Brown families. In addition, he is glad that periodically **he can still be the center of attention.**

DAD: - Well, that is about all the clues I can think of, right off the top of my head.

BOY: - That was some story! You must be exhausted.

GIRL: - Do you feel better now?

BOY: - I bet it was hard work writing the book, *If, I Did It.*

DAD: - I wrote it for you, kids. The $3,500,000 will help pay for college. It's a mean world for people like us, who suffer prejudice and bias and never get a break in life.

BOY: - Tell us straight up dad. Did you kill those people?

DAD: - No…no…no kids. I did not kill your mom. I'm only saying, if I did, here's how I did it.

GIRL: - Maybe we could write a book someday

BOY: - Like…"How Daddy Killed Mommy, If He Did It"?

GIRL: - No, that is silly and stupid.

DAD: - Yes, don't do anything silly and stupid. But, if you do, get the best lawyers your fame or money will buy.

GIRL: We love you dad. But why are you so sad?

DAD: I am sad, honey. I'm about to run out of ideas on how to keep my name and face in the news.

(Thought to myself) But, I will think of something.

O.J. Simpson and wife Nicole

SOURCES

Autopsy Report by the county coroner, Dr. Lakshmanan Sathyavagiswaran, 1994

Throwing the Books at O.J., by Gerald Posner (Esquire) Nov. 1996, after more than a dozen books on the trial, the verdict still does not fit.

Outrage: 5 Reasons Why O.J. Simpson Got Away with Murder, by Vincent Bugliosi (Seattle: Island Books.) 1997

"Courtroom Television Network Court TV Case files: O.J. Simpson, 1999. www.courttv.com/casefiles/simpson

The Trial of Orenthal James Simpson, by Doug Linder, 2000

Altered Dimension, at www.altereddimension.net

If, I Did It, a book by O.J. Simpson, publication by *Regan Books*, an imprint of HarperCollins Publishers. Publisher Judith Regan, 2006